Bella and Rosie
Trick-or-Treat

BY MICHÈLE DUFRESNE

Pioneer Valley Educational Press, Inc.

"I am hungry," said Bella.

"Me, too," said Rosie.

"Look," said Bella.
"Here is some candy.
 I love candy."

"Oh, no," said Rosie.
"The candy is for trick-or-treaters."

"We can trick-or-treat," said Bella.
"We can trick-or-treat for candy."

"Look," said Bella.
"I can be a wizard,
and you can be a witch."

"No," said Rosie.
"I am too scared."

"Look," said Rosie.
"I can be a queen,
and you can be a princess."

"No way," said Bella.
"No way!"

"Look," said Bella.
"I can be a pirate,
and you can be a cowboy."

"No! You can be a pirate,
and I can be a **cowgirl**," said Rosie.

"Come on," said Bella.
"We can trick-or-treat.
We can trick-or-treat for candy!"